KU-471-536

Something for Daddy

by Ted Dewan

Round the corner,
Not far away,
Bing begins another day.

Hello Bing.

Hello Flop.

Let's make something for Daddy.

What would Daddy like best?

A feathery thing?
A shiny thing?
A sparkly thing?
A shiny feathery sparkly thing?
YUP!

Here's what we need:

shiny things

feathers
sparkles

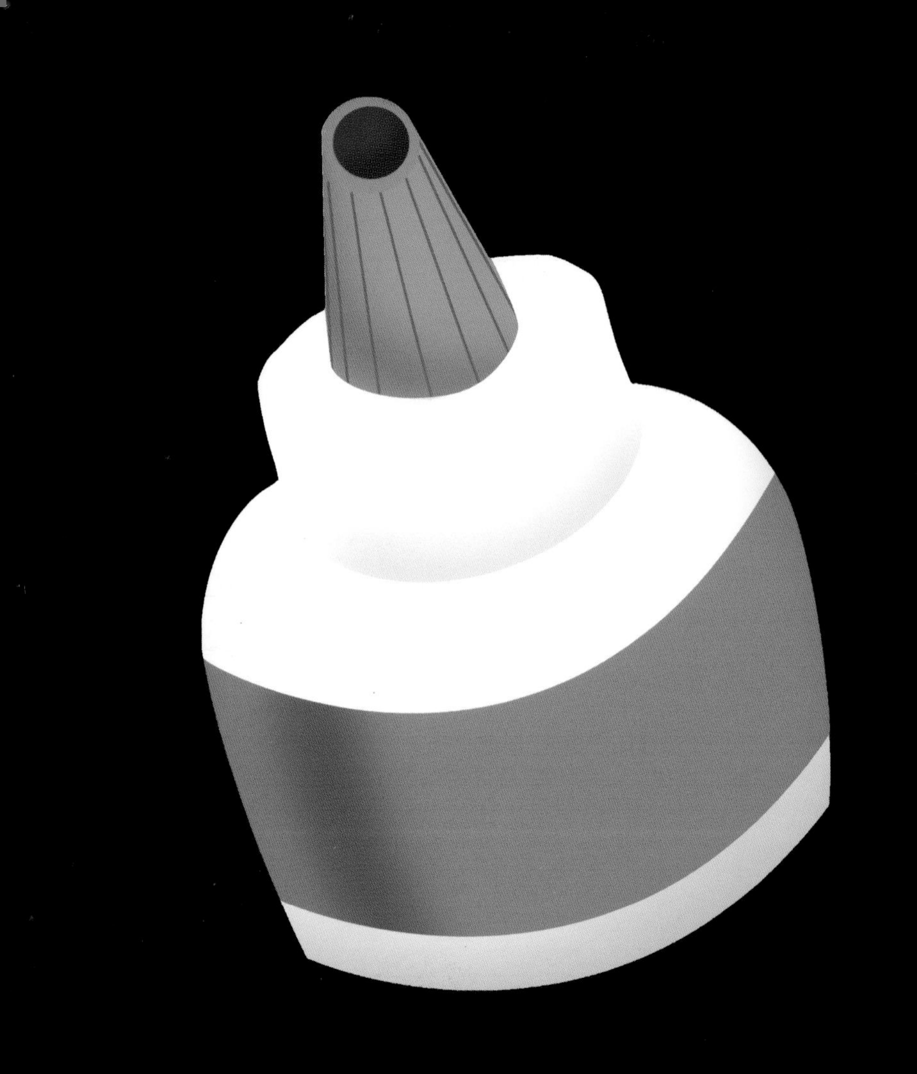

and a great
big
bottle of

goo

to stick them all
together.

First, let's do
shiny
things.
Squeeze
the goo

Stick on the shiny things.

Is it good?

Good for YOU, Bing Bunny.

Now some feathers.

Squeeze the goo.

Stick on the feathers.

Is it good?

YUP!

Good for YOU, Bing Bunny.

Now some sparkles.

Squeeze the goo.

Oops.
The goo is
stuck.
Squeeze
a little
more.
Just a bit
more.

P

K!

Oh no! Goo!

Don't worry, Bing.
It's no big thing.

Let's cover it all with...

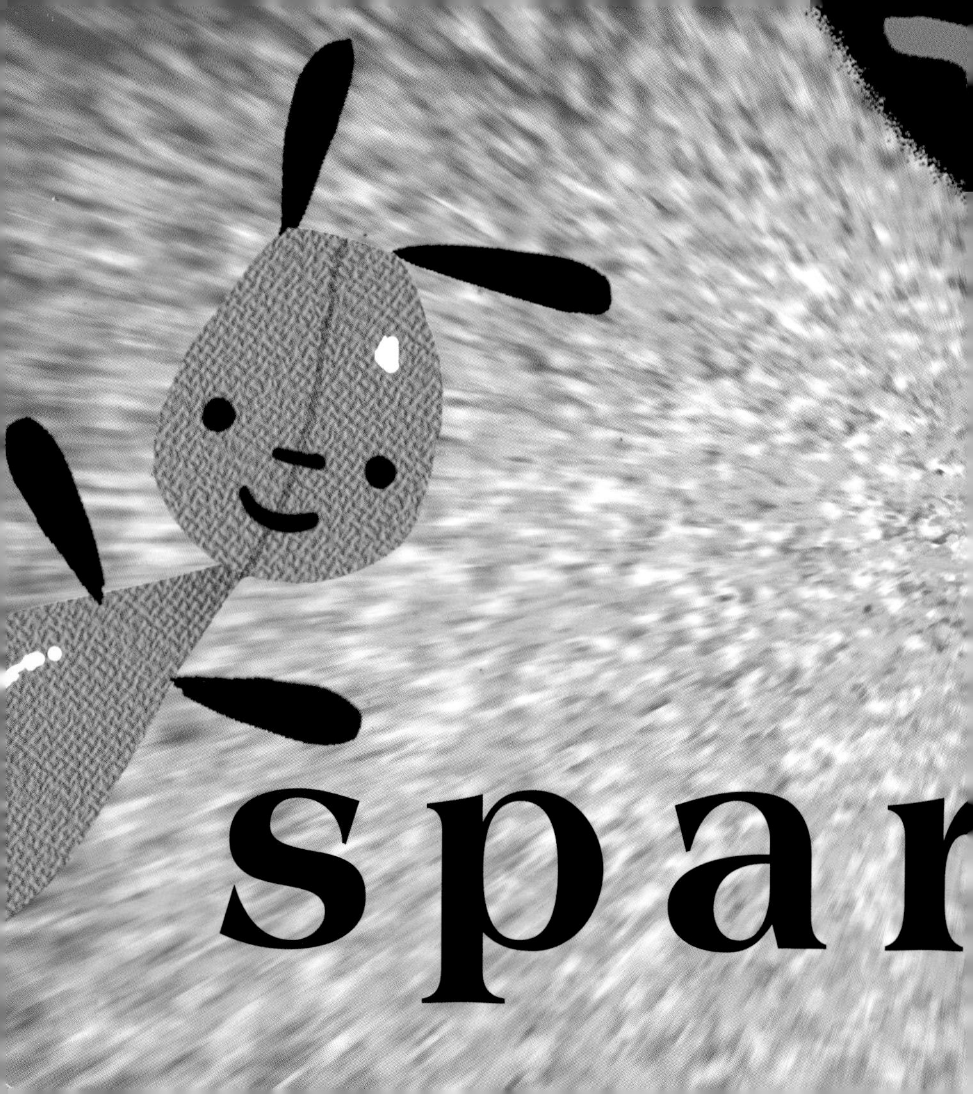
spar

kles!

It looks great!

Let's show it to Daddy.

Daddy will love
his shiny
feathery
sparkly
sticky-goo
thing...

because…

it's a Bing Thing.